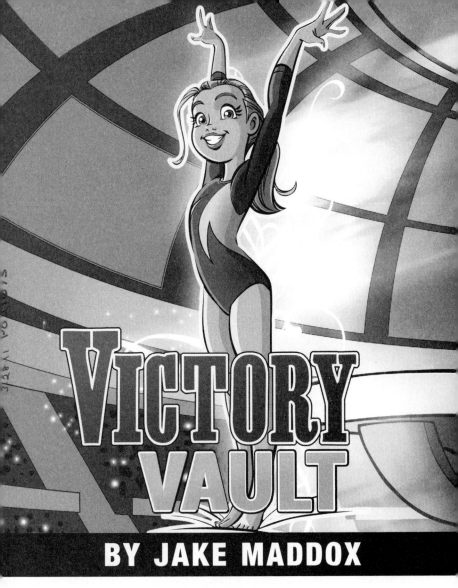

VICTORY VAULT

BY JAKE MADDOX

text by Emma Carlson Berne

illustrated by Pulsar Studio

Jake Maddox books are published by Stone Arch Books
A Capstone Imprint
151 Good Counsel Drive, P.O. Box 669
Mankato, Minnesota 56002
www.capstonepub.com

*Library of Congress Cataloging-in-Publication Data is available on the
Library of Congress website.*

Library Binding: 978-1-4342-2498-9

Summary: Kayla messes up her vault at an important gymnastics meet,
and the judges don't see it. But her best friend Chandra does. When
Chandra pressures her to tell the truth, Kayla has a decision to make.

Art Director/Graphic Desinger: Kay Fraser
Production Specialist: Michelle Biedscheid

Printed in the United States of America in Stevens Point, Wisconsin.
092010
005934WZS11

TABLE OF CONTENTS

CHAPTER 1

THE BEST GYMNAST

"All right, Starz! Vault work, everyone!"
Coach Steele called. He clapped his hands
loudly, signaling the end of the break.

On the bleachers, Kayla Meade shoved
her water bottle back into her gym bag.
"I don't know why he's making us do the
vault again," she muttered to her best
friend, Chandra Howard. "We've already
worked on our landings five times this
week." Kayla rolled her eyes.

"Coach is just trying to get us ready for the meet with the Newton Twisters tomorrow," Chandra said, pulling her hair into a tight ponytail. "Everyone keeps messing up. Except for you, of course." Chandra grinned at her friend. "I only wish my landings could look like yours, Miss Regional Gymnastics Champion 2010," she said. "You're the best gymnast here."

Kayla smiled a little. "Hey, I can't help being awesome," she said, laughing.

Chandra didn't laugh back. Instead, she just stared at Kayla for a moment. Then she shook her head and got up to join the other gymnasts at the vault.

Kayla slowly trailed to the end of the line. *I don't need to practice*, Kayla thought. *My landings are always perfect.*

She eyed Coach Steele. He was showing Madeline how to keep her back perfectly straight. Quietly, Kayla slipped her iPod out of the pocket of her warm-up jacket. She put one of the earphones in her ear.

Kayla watched as Chandra ran forward for her turn. "Go, Chandra!" Kayla shouted, clapping her hands. Chandra sprang into the air but flipped too late. As her feet landed on the mat, she lurched forward, taking a step out of position.

I would have stuck that landing, Kayla thought. *Her routine isn't even that hard.* Quietly, she turned up the volume on her iPod. She nodded her head in time to the music.

"Kayla!" Coach Steele called. "What are you doing?"

Kayla jumped and swiped the earphone from her ear. "Uh, nothing," she mumbled quietly.

Coach Steele walked over and held out his hand. "I think you'd better give me that," he said sternly.

Kayla placed the iPod in his palm. She could feel her face getting red.

"You need to pay attention during practice, Kayla," Coach Steele said, frowning. "You know that iPods aren't allowed."

Kayla didn't say anything.

Coach Steele sighed. "Why don't you show us your Yurchenko vault, Kayla? I'm sure it'll be perfect, since you obviously don't think you need to pay attention," he said.

"Fine," Kayla said. She slipped off her warm-up jacket and walked over to the end of the long mat. As she lined her toes up on the starting line, the other girls got quiet behind her.

Kayla straightened her back and ran forward at full speed. She threw her body into a round-off, and her feet hit the springboard with a loud *thwack*.

She arched immediately into a back handspring and felt her palms smack the surface of the vault table. She pushed off as hard as she could to get the height she needed to complete her post-flight.

Kayla's body soared in the air, twisting twice before coming back to the ground. With a *thump*, she landed solidly on both feet, knees bent, arms out to the side.

Straightening her knees, she raised her arms overhead, and then brought them down by her sides. Behind her, Kayla could hear the other gymnasts break into applause. She glanced over at Coach Steele. He was smiling and shaking his head.

"Another good one, Kayla," he called out.

Kayla grinned. Now maybe Coach would give her iPod back.

CHAPTER 2

A Tough Meet

By the end of practice, all of the Starz
were panting and sweaty. "Gather around,
girls," Coach Steele hollered. "As everyone
knows, tomorrow is our meet against the
Newton Twisters. Last year, they beat us
by ten points at this same meet. They're
extremely tough. That means we have
to be tough, too. I want everyone to stay
focused and alert. There's no room for
careless mistakes."

The coach looked out at the gymnasts in front of him. "That's it," he said. "Eat a good dinner, and go to bed early tonight. See you all tomorrow morning."

The girls walked toward the exit, lifting their bags over their shoulders and chattering excitedly to each other. Kayla had her hand on the heavy gym doors when she heard the coach's voice coming from behind her.

"Kayla, could you come here, please?" he called.

Kayla glanced over at Chandra. "I'll wait outside," Chandra said.

Kayla walked over to the bleachers, where Coach Steele was sitting. He patted the hard wooden bench, and Kayla sat down. He looked her right in the eyes.

"Your vault routine was excellent, Kayla," he said. "You're a talented gymnast. In fact, you're one of the best on the team. But you still have to work hard and pay attention during practice."

Kayla felt annoyed. The vault routine was so easy. She didn't need any more practice. But she could never say these things to her coach. Instead, she just nodded silently.

Coach Steele smiled. "Okay. I'll see you tomorrow," he said. Kayla jumped off the bench as if it had suddenly turned red hot.

Outside, Chandra was waiting in the parking lot. Bright sunshine glinted off puddles of rainwater. As they trudged across the soggy grass of the athletic fields, Chandra was quiet.

Kayla glanced over at her friend. Chandra was staring down at the ground as she walked. "What's the matter?" Kayla asked.

Chandra shrugged her shoulders and played with the zipper on her jacket. "I'm just a little nervous about the meet tomorrow," she said. "My vault landing wasn't very good today. And you heard what Coach Steele said. The Twisters are a really tough team to beat. Aren't you worried too?"

"What do I have to be worried about?" Kayla asked. "The routines are so easy. I could stick that vault landing in my sleep. Besides, I bet Coach is just trying to scare us. He's so serious. He acts like gymnastics is the only important thing in the entire world."

The girls stopped in front of Chandra's house. "You know, gymnastics isn't as easy for everyone as it is for you, Kayla," Chandra said quietly. "I have to practice ten times as hard as you do. Even then, I'm not nearly as good."

Kayla gave Chandra a hug. "You're thinking about it too much," Kayla said. "Stop worrying! Your landings are going to be awesome, okay?"

"Maybe," Chandra said slowly. "Your landings will be awesome, that's for sure."

"Well, you're probably right about that," Kayla replied, laughing. She hugged Chandra. Then she waved as her friend went into the house and shut the door.

CHAPTER 3

A Hard Landing

When Kayla got to the gym the next morning, the normally empty bleachers were filled with parents and other family members. The judges' table stood against one wall with a microphone in front. The sound of the crowd echoed off the walls.

"There are the Twisters," Chandra whispered to Kayla, pointing to the other end of the gym. "They do look tough, just like Coach said."

The Twisters stood in a tight group around their coach. They all wore matching white leotards with red and gold sequined stripes down the sides.

At the other end of the gym, one of the judges leaned toward the microphone. She cleared her throat. Everyone fell silent. "We are ready to begin the meet," the judge announced. "Balance beam is first. Twisters and Starz, please take your places."

Kayla watched across the gym as Chandra took her place at the balance beam. Chandra quickly boosted herself up onto the four-inch-wide beam. As required, her routine was a mixture of dance and acrobatic elements combined with gymnastics. Chandra launched into her first skill, a full turn on one foot followed by a cross handstand.

She landed gracefully, walked down the beam, and launched into a front somersault. As soon as Chandra landed, she immediately went into a back handspring.

Next, Chandra completed a low cartwheel down onto the beam and lifted her body into a handstand. As Kayla watched, Chandra completed a wolf jump, followed by a split jump. She was careful to extend both legs completely in opposite directions.

Kayla wasn't scheduled to compete until later in the meet. So as Chandra finished her routine, Kayla's mind started to wander. She stretched back on the bleachers, crossing her legs in front of her. She tapped her fingers on the bleacher seat and wished she had her iPod.

It's so boring watching everyone do these little baby routines over and over, Kayla thought. *They act so serious, like it's the Olympics or something.*

The meet dragged on. Sometimes the Starz pulled ahead by a few points. Sometimes the Twisters were ahead. Kayla felt like a robot as she performed her floor routine, followed by the uneven bars and balance beam.

Finally, she heard the judge's voice. "The next gymnasts to vault should now meet in the corner of the gym," the judge called.

Kayla looked over at Chandra's anxious face. "Don't worry!" Kayla whispered. "This is going to be easy."

"Yeah, for you," Chandra whispered back as they walked toward the vault area.

"Chandra Howard," the announcer called. Chandra stepped forward to the white line. Kayla watched as her friend ran hard down the mat. Chandra thumped the springboard solidly and smacked the vault with both hands. Then she soared into the air, twisted, and landed solidly on her feet.

"Woo-hoo!" Kayla called. The other Starz clapped and whistled. Chandra ran back to the group, her face beaming. She and Kayla watched as the other gymnasts took their turns.

Finally, only Kayla was left to vault for her team. The Twisters and the Starz were only separated by a few points. Kayla's score would decide the winner. *It's all up to me now*, Kayla thought. *Piece of cake.*

"Kayla Meade," the announcer's voice boomed.

Kayla stepped forward, her back perfectly straight. She raised one arm straight up and then slapped it down by her side to signal to the judges that she was ready. She turned toward the vault. It looked very far away.

Kayla started running as fast as she could, pumping her arms. She hit the springboard with both feet, but to her surprise, her *thump* didn't sound as loud as usual. Kayla fought to launch herself high enough to complete her handspring, but she could tell she wasn't uncurling fast enough.

She landed with a *whump.* Then, to her horror, she felt herself lose balance and pitch forward. Without thinking, she stuck one foot out in front of her. She fought to keep herself from falling.

Before she could stop it, she hopped the other foot a few inches to steady herself. Kayla's heart sank. With that one movement, she had ruined her routine and her team's chance at winning the meet.

CHAPTER 4

KAYLA'S DECISION

Kayla could hardly bear to look at the judges. Moving both feet on a landing would definitely cost her points. How could she have messed up so badly? That landing was her best move.

Sadly, Kayla raised her arms, then lowered them, signaling the end of the routine. She lifted her gaze just enough to see the judges' faces. To her surprise, they were smiling and nodding their heads.

Confused, Kayla turned back to her team. Instead of watching her, they were all looking at the uneven bars. Only Chandra stood off to one side, gazing at Kayla. No one else seemed to have noticed what had just happened.

Kayla walked over to the group. "What's going on?" she asked Chandra.

"One of the Twisters fell off the bars during her routine," Chandra replied, pointing across the gym. "She came down pretty hard." Near the uneven bars, Kayla could see the Twisters coach and a paramedic kneeling next to a gymnast. They were checking her for injuries.

"Oh no," Kayla said. "I hope she's okay." Suddenly, the audience applauded as the Twisters gymnast nodded and slowly stood up. She was going to be fine.

Kayla glanced around and leaned over to Chandra. "Did you see me mess up my landing?" she whispered.

"Yeah, I saw you step out," Chandra said. "But just as you landed, that girl came crashing down, and everyone looked. I think even the judges looked."

"The judges were smiling after the routine," Kayla said. "But they had to have seen my landing."

"I'm not so sure about that," Chandra replied. "Look, here come the judges' scores." Both girls looked up. The big scoreboard lit up with the words "Kayla Meade, Vault, 9.5."

The rest of the team started cheering. They gathered around Kayla, patting her arms and back.

"Nice work, Kayla!" Coach Steele yelled. He reached over to slap Kayla's hand. "That score puts us over the top," he added. "The Starz win!"

Kayla just stared at her celebrating teammates. They all thought she'd performed a perfect routine. No one but Chandra knew she hadn't. Even the judges didn't know.

For a long moment, Kayla stood frozen in place. She knew she needed to tell the coach what had happened. Kayla started to walk toward him. But before she could say anything, music blared over the loudspeakers.

"Starz, please approach the podium," the head judge announced through the microphone.

The team marched up to the front of the gym, and Kayla accepted the big silver trophy the judge handed her. "Kayla, as the tie-breaker for the meet, the trophy is yours to keep," Coach Steele said.

Kayla turned around. On the other side of the gym, the Twisters were looking down at their feet and talking to each other quietly.

Kayla looked down at the trophy in her hands. Etched on the shining surface were the words *Southeast Regional Gymnastic Champions*. She hugged the trophy to her chest. The silver felt heavy and warm in her hands.

Slowly, Kayla turned to face the audience. She raised the trophy up over her head, and the audience cheered.

Kayla beamed. She looked around at the smiling faces of her teammates. Chandra was standing off to one side, frowning. Kayla gave her a big grin. But Chandra didn't smile back.

CHAPTER 5

"You Don't Deserve it!"

Kayla shoved open the heavy locker room door. She was still clutching the trophy with one hand. Inside, the big room echoed with the excited chatter of her teammates.

Kayla set the trophy down on a bench and pulled a pair of warm-up pants over her leotard. Just then, she spotted Chandra sitting on a bench, putting on her sneakers. Kayla slid onto the bench next to her.

"That was a great meet, huh?" Kayla said.

Chandra didn't look up.

"What's the matter?" Kayla asked, putting her arm around her friend's shoulders.

Chandra pushed Kayla's arm away and looked up. Kayla was surprised to see anger in her face. "This isn't right," Chandra whispered.

"What's not right?" Kayla asked.

Chandra looked around the crowded locker room. She pulled Kayla into a quiet corner by the sinks. Then she turned to face Kayla, hands on her hips. "You don't deserve that trophy," Chandra said. "You messed up your landing. You and I both know it."

Kayla's eyes widened. "What are you talking about?" she replied. "It's not my fault the judges didn't see the landing. That's their job."

Chandra shook her head. "They should have seen the landing, but that doesn't matter," she said. "You're accepting a trophy you didn't earn."

"So, what do you want to me to do?" Kayla asked. She snorted. "Give it back?"

She was joking, but Chandra nodded. "Yeah. I think you should give the trophy back, and tell Coach Steele what happened," she told Kayla.

"What!" Kayla exclaimed. "No way! The trophy is mine, fair and square. Besides, the scores have already been recorded. The judges aren't going to change them."

"Maybe not, but that's not the point," Chandra replied. "You're lying if you take the trophy and don't say anything."

Kayla threw her hands up in the air. "How can I be lying? I never told a lie!" she almost shouted. A couple of girls glanced over. Kayla lowered her voice. "Look, no one knows what happened. Let's just forget about it," she said quietly.

Chandra crossed her arms over her chest. "I didn't think you were that kind of person, Kayla," she finally said. "But you've been slacking off in practice all year. You act like you don't even care about the team. Just because you're the best doesn't mean you don't have to follow the rules."

Open-mouthed, Kayla stared at her friend. She'd never heard Chandra talk this way before.

Chandra turned away. "I'm not friends with liars," she said as she crossed the room. She plucked her gym bag from the bench and threw it over her shoulder. She slammed the locker room door closed behind her, leaving Kayla standing alone in the center of the room.

CHAPTER 6

Fair and Square

The next morning, Kayla waited under the big oak tree at the end of her street. She and Chandra always met there to walk to school together.

Kayla glanced at her watch. Homeroom started in five minutes. She had to leave soon, or she would be late. Kayla stared up and down the sidewalk, hoping to see Chandra heading toward her. But all she saw was the empty street.

Kayla glanced at her watch one more time. Maybe Chandra had overslept. Kayla darted out from under the tree branches and ran as fast as she could the rest of the way to school.

She couldn't believe her eyes when she slid into her seat in homeroom. Chandra was already in the classroom, staring down at a notebook. She glanced up quickly and then looked down again when she saw Kayla staring at her. Kayla shot her a questioning look, but there was no time to talk before Mrs. Cameron started class.

After class, Kayla grabbed the sleeve of Chandra's sweatshirt as her friend tried to slip by. "Chandra, wait!" Kayla pleaded. She couldn't hide the hurt in her voice. "Where were you this morning?" she asked. "I waited for you."

Chandra just stared at the gray linoleum floor. "I told you, Kayla," she mumbled, not looking up. "I don't want to talk to you. Not after what happened at the meet. I'm sorry. I can't help it." She looked up quickly. Kayla could see that her eyes were full of tears.

Kayla reached her hand out to her friend. "Chandra, come on, it's not that big of a deal," Kayla started to say. But Chandra pulled away and hurried down the hall.

Kayla dragged herself through the rest of the day. Her classes seemed way longer than usual. All she wanted to do was put her head down on the desk. She couldn't believe Chandra wouldn't speak to her. As soon as the final bell rang, Kayla jumped up from her desk and ran home.

She opened the front door quietly. Mom was singing to herself in the kitchen. Kayla tried to sneak up the stairs to her room, but she heard her mom turn the radio down. "Honey, is that you?" Mom called.

"Yeah! I'm just going upstairs for a while. I have a lot of homework," Kayla called back. She tried to make her voice sound normal, but she could tell that it was a little shaky.

She was lying facedown on her bed when her mom opened the door. Mom sat down and stroked Kayla's hair. "What's the matter, honey?" Mom asked in a quiet voice.

Kayla rolled over. Mom passed her a box of tissues from the bedside table. "Nothing," Kayla said, sniffling. She blew her nose loudly.

Mom smiled and patted Kayla's hand. "Okay," she said, but she didn't get up from the bed. She just sat there until Kayla sighed.

"Well, if you really want to know, I'm in a big fight with Chandra, okay?" Kayla finally muttered. Just saying those words made her feel like she was going to cry all over again. She buried her face in the pillow.

"What's the problem, sweetie?" her mom asked.

"Nothing. It's just something that happened at the meet yesterday, okay?" Kayla said.

"Do you want to tell me what happened?" Mom asked. "Maybe it would help if we talked about it."

Kayla sighed again, but she told her mom what had happened at the meet, including her argument with Chandra in the locker room. Then she finished, "And she wants me to tell Coach Steele what happened, but I didn't do anything wrong! I'm not a liar. That trophy is mine, fair and square."

Mom was quiet after Kayla was done talking. "Actually, honey, I think you're both right," she finally said.

"How can we both be right?" Kayla asked.

"Well, you're right because it really was the judges who made a mistake," Mom explained. "They missed your landing and should have taken points off your score. But the judges are in charge. If they gave you the trophy, it's yours, fair and square."

"Exactly!" Kayla exclaimed. "It's not my fault they didn't see it. I didn't lie."

"But Chandra is right, too," Mom continued. "Some things are more important than being 'fair and square.' Like being honest, even though you didn't exactly do anything wrong. In your heart, you know you shouldn't have won that trophy. You need to tell the coach the truth. He'll decide if you should tell the judges."

Kayla was silent for a long time after her mom finished talking. She hadn't thought about it like that. Finally, she sat up and brushed her hair out of her eyes. "Thanks, Mom," she said, giving her mom a hug. "What's for dinner?" she asked.

Mom smiled. "Roast chicken," she said, getting up from the bed.

Kayla climbed out from under the comforter and stood up. "I'll be right down," she said. "I just have to make a phone call first."

CHAPTER 7

A Perfect Landing

Shooom! A Newton Twister released
the high bars and soared into the air in
a corner of the arena. Across the gym,
another girl was practicing her floor routine
while spectators watched.

The big gym was packed with all of
the local teams, gathered for the regional
qualifying final. The bleachers were filled,
and the judges sat behind their long table
on the sidelines.

At one end, the Starz gathered around Coach Steele. He examined the list of events on his clipboard. "Okay, first up we have Madeline on uneven bars, Lauren doing the floor routine, Chandra on balance beam, and Kayla on vault," he said. "Let's get going, girls. Start warming up."

Kayla barely heard the coach's words. This past week had been the longest of her life. Chandra still wasn't speaking to her. All Kayla could think about was the whole mess at the last meet. Usually, she was full of nervous, bubbly energy before a meet. But this time, she felt steadier. She knew what had to be done, and she was prepared to do it.

Hopefully, by the end of today, everything will be different, Kayla told herself.

She glanced at Chandra. Her friend was sitting quietly at the edge of the bleachers, intently studying a scrap of paper in her hand.

Kayla took a deep breath. *It's now or never*, she told herself as she walked toward her friend. She stood in front of Chandra nervously for a second.

"What are you reading?" Kayla finally asked. Her voice sounded small.

"It's my balance beam routine," Chandra replied without looking up. "I'm up next."

"Oh right, that's always hard to remember," Kayla said.

Chandra didn't answer. She kept her eyes fixed on the scrap of paper in her hands.

"So, um, there's going to be a . . . special event . . . right after we're all done competing. Are you going to stick around after you're through with the balance beam?" Kayla asked, shifting her weight from foot to foot. She wiped her sweaty palms on the sides of her leotard.

"I don't know," Chandra said, finally glancing up at Kayla. "I might have to go to a dentist appointment."

"Chandra Howard, balance beam," the announcer called. Both girls jumped.

"Well, I guess that's me," Chandra said, getting up from the bench. She slipped off her warm-up jacket and tucked the scrap of paper into the leg of her leotard. "See you."

"I hope you can stick around!" Kayla called to her friend's back.

* * *

Kayla stood at the edge of the long blue mat. Everyone else had finished vaulting. Only Kayla was left. She concentrated on breathing deeply. Slowly, the whole gym melted away. Soon, all Kayla could hear was the sound of her own blood rushing through her veins. She lifted her arm to salute the table of judges.

Kayla ran forward, pumping her arms. She hit the springboard as hard as she could. This time, the *thump* felt just right under her feet. She felt the smooth leather under her palms as her hands hit the vault.

She pushed off as hard as she could, launching her body into the air. Before she could think, Kayla found herself soaring through the air, twisting and flipping before coming back to the mat.

She could tell as soon as her feet hit the mat that the landing was going to be perfect. She brought her weight squarely onto the balls of her feet, then her heels, without moving even a centimeter. She'd stuck a perfect landing.

As Kayla raised her arms to signal the end of her routine, the crowd roared. "Go, Kayla!" Mom yelled above everyone else.

Kayla walked slowly back to the group. Chandra was still sitting on the bleachers, not looking up. The announcer's voice boomed over the loudspeaker. "Thank you to all our teams today," he said. "Please wait while the judges add up the scores."

The Starz buzzed with excitement. Kayla exchanged a glance with Coach Steele, then turned and walked toward the judges' table. Coach Steele followed closely behind.

The coach leaned over and whispered to one of the judges. The judge's eyes widened in surprise. He thought for a minute. Then he leaned over and whispered something to the other judges.

Kayla watched anxiously from a few feet away. She couldn't hear what they were saying. Then the judge nodded. He held out the microphone in Kayla's direction, and she walked slowly up to the table.

CHAPTER 8

A True Star

The crowd grew quiet. Kayla turned to face them. Her heart hammered in her ears. Coach gave her an encouraging nod.

Kayla held the microphone close to her mouth. "Um . . ." she began. She took a deep breath. "This is really hard," Kayla said. Her voice shook. She paused and swallowed. A sea of faces stared at her. "At the last meet . . ." She cleared her throat. "At the last meet, I . . . made a mistake."

A little murmur ran through the crowd. The Starz gasped. Kayla caught a glimpse of the Twisters in the corner. Their eyes were locked on her.

Kayla steeled herself and went on. "I didn't stick the landing in my vault routine, but I didn't get points taken away."

The judges glanced at each other. The crowd was silent now, waiting.

"Because of my score, the Starz won the meet, and I was given the trophy," Kayla said. "But I know I should have said something about the mistake." She stared down at her toes. Then she gathered her strength and looked up. "The truth is that I wanted the trophy for myself. I thought I deserved it, even though I didn't." She paused. In the bleachers, she could see her mother smiling.

"I realize now that even though something is technically yours, it doesn't always mean it's okay to keep it," she continued. Kayla looked right at Chandra as she spoke. Chandra's mouth was hanging open.

Kayla turned to the judges. "If it's possible, my coach and I would like to return the trophy. We would like to have my score corrected to show the mistake in the routine," she said.

Kayla turned to her mom and waved. Her mother made her way down from the bleachers with the trophy in her hand. She gave it to Kayla, along with a little hug. Kayla put it on the judges' table, then backed away until she bumped into Coach Steele. He laid a reassuring hand on her shoulder. "Nice work," he whispered.

Kayla waited nervously. For what seemed like years, the judges muttered to each other at their table. The audience was silent. Finally, one of the judges leaned forward and cleared his throat.

"According to the rulebook, a recorded score can be changed only in the case of obvious cheating. While we're glad Kayla Meade told the truth, her score can't be changed," the judge said.

Kayla's shoulders sagged. "It's okay," Coach Steele said. "All we could do is try." Slowly, Kayla made her way back to the Starz, holding the trophy in one hand.

As she neared the group, Chandra pushed through the crowd. She threw her arms around her friend. "That was amazing, Kayla!" she said happily. "You're so brave. When did you tell the coach?"

"I called him last week and told him the whole thing," Kayla said. "But our plan didn't work. They won't take the trophy back."

"That doesn't matter," Chandra said. "What matters is that you tried." She linked her arm through Kayla's. "I knew you could do it."

Kayla grinned back at her best friend. She was relieved they weren't fighting anymore. "But what about this?" she asked, holding up the trophy.

Chandra thought a minute. "I've got an idea," she exclaimed. "What about giving it to them?" She pointed to the Twisters across the gym. "It would have been theirs anyway if your score had been recorded right," she said.

Kayla raised her eyebrows. "Yeah, you're right," she said. She ran her hand over the trophy. "Okay, let's ask the rest of the team." She turned to the Starz. Now that they had finished competing, the gymnasts were all sitting on the floor and bleachers, talking, rubbing their legs, and tying up their hair.

"Girls!" Kayla called. "Listen up! Chandra and I have a little plan we want to run by you." She explained what they wanted to do. Their teammates all nodded in agreement.

"Let's do it," Madeline said. She got to her feet, followed by the rest of the team. With Kayla and Chandra in the lead, they marched to the other side of the gym toward the Twisters. Kayla carried the trophy with her.

The Twisters looked up in surprise as the Starz approached. Kayla handed the trophy to the Twisters captain. "I know the judges said we couldn't officially change the scores. But we want to give you this," Kayla said. "It really is yours. Your team would have won if my score had been recorded right."

The captain smiled. "Thanks," she said. "I can't believe you'd do this."

Kayla smiled at Chandra, who stood by her side. "I can't either," Kayla said, throwing her arm around Chandra's shoulders. "But I had some really good coaching."

ABOUT THE AUTHOR

Emma Carlson Berne has written more than a dozen books for children and young adults, including teen romance novels, biographies, and history books. She lives in Cincinnati, Ohio with her husband, Aaron, her son, Henry, and her dog, Holly.

ABOUT THE ILLUSTRADOR

Pulsar Studio is a collection of artists from Argentina who work to bring editorial projects to life. They work with companies from different parts of the world designing characters, short stories for children, textbooks, art for book covers, comics, licensed art, and more. Images are their means of expression.

GLOSSARY

alert (uh-LURT)—paying attention

anxious (ANGK-shuhss)—worried

etched (ECHD)—engraved or drawn on metal or glass

extend (ek-STEND)—to make something longer or bigger; to stretch out

gracefully (GRAYSS-fuh-lee)—an elegant way of moving

obvious (OB-vee-uhss)—something that is easy to see or understand

paramedic (pa-ruh-MED-ik)—a person trained to give emergency medical treatment but who is not a doctor or a nurse

routine (roo-TEEN)—a regular way or pattern of doing things

technically (TEK-nuh-kuh-lee)—according to the given rules

DISCUSSION QUESTIONS

1. At the end of the book, the judges won't take back the trophy, even after Kayla speaks up. Talk about how you would feel if you were a member of the opposing team, the Twisters.

2. Chandra gets upset with Kayla for not telling the truth about her landing, but Kayla doesn't think she did anything wrong. Who do you think was right and why? Talk about both sides of the argument.

3. What do you think the hardest gymnastics event is? Talk about your choice. What do you think makes it so difficult?

WRITING PROMPTS

1. Kayla and Chandra get in a fight about Kayla's mistake at the gymnastics meet. Have you ever gotten in a fight with a friend? Write about that experience. How did you resolve your argument?

2. Write about a time someone helped you see the other side of an argument. What happened? How did the person help you?

3. Imagine you were in Kayla's position, and the judges gave you the trophy, even though you technically didn't deserve it. Write about what you would have done.

MORE ABOUT
WOMEN'S GYMNASTICS

Gymnastics is a sport that requires incredible strength and flexibility. Women's gymnastics is made up of four events: vault, balance beam, floor exercise, and uneven bars.

• **Vault** — A good vault begins with a strong run. A gymnast must sprint down a runway, jump with either feet or hands onto a springboard, and then push hard off the vault table. The best vaulters are often the strongest. They must have enough power to push high off the table and complete their rotation.

• **Balance beam** — The balance beam is often considered the most difficult event. Gymnasts must have excellent balance to stay on the four-inch beam. The goal is to perform a routine that makes it seem like the gymnast is on the floor instead of the beam.

• **Floor exercise** — The floor routine is often most popular, since it reflects a gymnast's personality. The routine is set to music and must use the entire floor area. Floor exercise uses a spring floor, which lets gymnasts go higher during tumbling passes. The gymnast must use a combination of dance and tumbling elements in her routine.

• **Uneven bars** — In this event, a gymnast performs a routine on two bars set at different heights. The gymnast swings from one bar to the other while performing handstands, flips, and twists. This requires concentration, coordination, and split-second timing, as well as great upper-body strength. The most difficult elements are release moves, when a gymnast releases one bar and transitions to the other.

More **Fabulous** Sports Books!

FIND THESE AND OTHER
JAKE MADDOX BOOKS

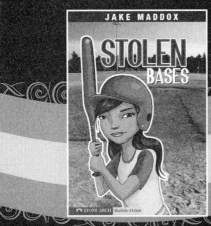

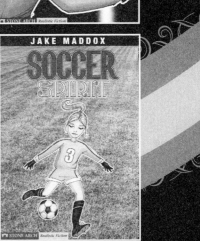

WWW.CAPSTONEPUB.COM